HATARI! DANGER!

Life among the animals of Kenya's Masai Mara

Jackson Liaram
and Mary Bowman-Kruhm

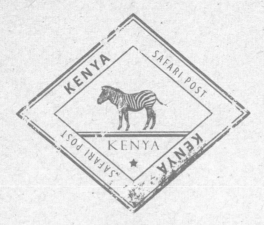

Reycraft Books
55 Fifth Avenue
New York, NY 10003
Reycraftbooks.com

Reycraft Books is a trade imprint and trademark of Newmark Learning, LLC.

Library of Congress Control Number: 2021924952

ISBN: 978-1-4788-7054-8

Photo Credits: Page iA,5: Jackson Liaram; Page 4B,4C,191: Carl L. Kruhm, Jr.; Page 6A-7A: Xplorer Maps, LLC (Missoula, MT); Page 19H: PhotoStock-Israel/Alamy; Page 154H: Science History Images/Alamy; All other images from Getty Images and Shutterstock.

Printed in Dongguan, China. 8557/0222/18798
10 9 8 7 6 5 4 3 2 1

First Edition Paperback published by Reycraft Books 2022.

TABLE OF CONTENTS

Dedicated to:

My older brother Nterere for mentoring my herding skills
and
my family members Susan Nekwama,
Mereso Sanau, Lesiamon, Maripet, Nadupoi, Naisiae,
and Sanare with the hope that this book brings
excitement of an Author in the family for the first time.
J.M.L.

The Unitarian Universalist Congregation of
Frederick & Rotary Clubs in Maryland
that dug a well for Oltorotua
and
Olivia, Josie, & Amelia Wiesman,
MJ & Grace Petrilli,
Kennedy and Avery Redmond,
with the hope that they love Kenya as I do
M.B-K.

1

INTRODUCTION

Jambo!

My name is Jackson Minteeng Liaram, and I am a safari guide. Jambo is a Swahili word that means hello. In Kenya, where we speak both Swahili and English, we tell visitors "Jambo" many times when we take them on safari. Safari is another Swahili word and means trip or journey. On safari, guides help visitors learn about our exciting country.

I am a Maasai, one of Kenya's smallest tribal groups. We are often the face of Kenya you see in pictures. The men hold spears and wear a red and blue or black cloth called a shuka.

We Maasai belong to one of the world's most exciting cultures. Wildlife, livestock, and people live in harmony in Maasailand, East Africa. Maasailand refers to land owned by the Maasai tribe, regardless of the country in which we live. On a map, Maasailand stretches from outside Nairobi, Kenya's capital city, south to Ngorongoro Crater in Tanzania, east to the slopes of Mt. Kilimanjaro, and west 50 miles from the Masai Mara Game Reserve.

The Masai Mara Game Reserve covers 583 square miles. It is a huge open park that protects our precious wildlife, which are valuable to us in many ways. Kenyans refer to both the game reserve and the nearby land where the Maasai live as "the Mara."

Since wildlife freely roams in the park, and humans only visit, we Maasai live outside the park. Several compounds, separated from each other by about a half-mile, make a village. My village is Oltorotua. It is near the border with Tanzania. I was born in 1983 and am a brother to 18 other boys and girls from my father's three wives. I am proud to have a wife, Susan, and four children.

Roads in Oltorotua are few; people walk. Cellphones now make staying in touch with other villagers easier. Easier than a loud shout or blowing a horn. And much easier than walking. A hike in the bush is not for faint-hearts, since it brings the risk of meeting a wild animal. That can mean *Hatari*—danger in Swahili. To attend school, I walked five miles early in the morning and again back in the evening, and many times, I encountered wildlife.

Both wild animals and the domestic animals my family raises have been a big part of my life. I have herded my family's cattle, sheep, and goats since I was little. When I was about eight, my older brother Nterere told me to throw stones at the wild animals I saw. He thought they were eating too much grass and so our sheep would have nothing to eat.

Then I saw a ranger wearing a green uniform walking toward me. He asked, "Why are you threatening wildlife?" I quickly turned and ran toward home. The ranger was faster. He caught me and explained that wild animals are important to us. Because I was afraid of the ranger, I listened very carefully. I remember this well. I began to love wildlife and realize their value.

These animals have been part of our lives for as long as the history of the Maasai people. I like living and working close to them, but animals roaming the plains of Kenya are not like those in a zoo. They are some of the largest, smartest, deadliest wildlife on earth.

Read on. Enjoy, but remember: *Hatari! Danger!*

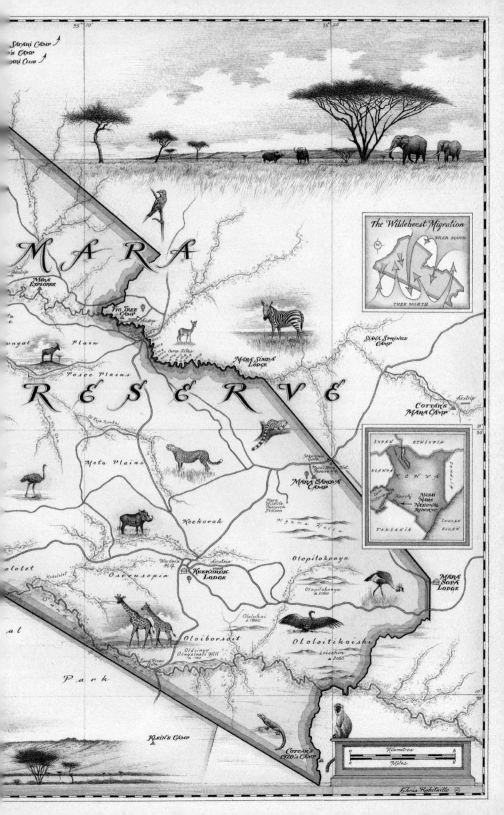

SAFARI CAMP

'S CAMP

ARI CLUB

M A R A

Airstrip

MARA
EXPLORER

FIG TREE
CAMP

Plain

Posee Plains

Camp Kifaru

R E S E R V E

MARA SIMBAS
LODGE

SIANA SPRINGS
CAMP

COTTAR'S
MARA CAMP

Airstrip

Ol Keju Ronkai

Meta Plains

Sekenani
Gate

Masai Mara Nat.
Reserve H.Q.

MARA SAROVA
CAMP

Mara
Wildlife
Research Station

Keekorok

Ngama Hills

Oserusopia

Wardens
H.Q.

Airstrip

KEEKOROK
LODGE

Ololet

Keboloet

Kebolet

Mara

Olopitokonya

Olopitokonya
▲ 2060

MARA
SOPA
LODGE

Ololukai
▲ 1860

Ololoitikoishe

Oloiborsoit

Oldoinyo
Olngainali Hill
1720

Loisekin
▲ 2060

al

Sand River
Gate

P a r k

KLEIN'S CAMP

COTTAR'S
1920's CAMP

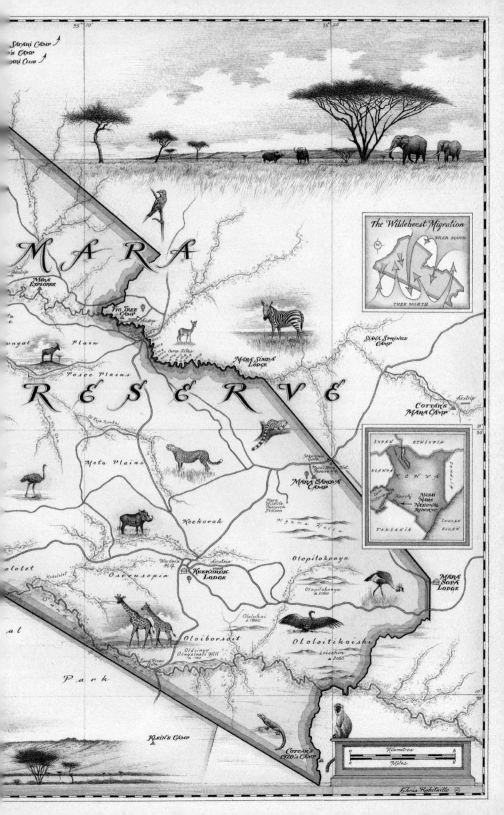
The Wildebeest Migration

TREK SOUTH

TREK NORTH

SUDAN   ETHIOPIA

UGANDA   K E N Y A

SOMALIA

Lake
Victoria

Nairobi

MASAI
MARA
NATIONAL
RESERVE

INDIAN
OCEAN

TANZANIA

Kilometres

Miles

Chris Robitaille

KEEKOROK AIRSTRIP

MASAI MARA NATIONAL RESERVE

Longitude – e35'15"33"
Latitude – s01'35"10"
Altitude – 5570 ft

2

HATARI! DANGER! LION!

When I was young, many lions roamed near our village. Let me tell you about a lion scare I once had.

It was the darkest night ever. The kind of night the Maasai say is so black that you cannot see someone pinching your eyeball. My brother Nterere and I were sleeping in our orripie. An orripie is a small guardhouse, where we stayed at night to protect our cattle, sheep, and goats. From the orripie we could see all the animals. The cows were in the large area around our circle of houses. The sheep and goats were in their kraal. You may call this small fenced-in area a corral.

The fire was lit, as that was my father's rule. We were wet from an evening rain. As soon as our clothes dried, we fell into a deep sleep.

The fire burned off. Suddenly, in my dream I heard a lion growl. I ignored it. I sensed it again and again. Then I awoke. No dream.

Hatari! Danger! LION!

I shouted into Nterere's ear—"Wake up! Wake up!"

It was not too long before the roar of the lion exploded everywhere. It was the loudest, longest drumbeat I have ever heard. It sounded as if the lion was laughing at us. Then we heard growls.

I couldn't do anything. I was scared out of my senses.

Nterere boldly snatched up his sword. It was hanging on the wall, over his head, easy to grab. I wanted to yell, but my voice stuck in my throat.

I could hear the goats scream. A sure sign things were very bad. More growls from the lion. I could not tell the direction the growls were coming from. They seemed as if they came from everywhere.

In the dark night, Nterere couldn't see where to direct his sword. But the goats kept screaming. And screaming.

Finally my voice became loud enough to reach 50 meters, to the closest house. Our elder brother Moniko came, holding his spear. In his other hand was a burning olive branch, which provides a soft glow and doesn't smoke or go out easily in the wind. It sparkled with the wind but stayed lit. He had jumped over the spiky thorn fence and landed in the kraal, only a foot away from the lion's tail.

In the night we could not know if it was a male or female lion. Now I can tell the different sound each makes, but, as a young boy, I could not hear the difference. I knew only that the lion growled at Moniko in the dark night as it chewed soft goat meat.

Moniko knew it was important to save the live animals in the kraal from the mouth of the lion. If he threw his spear, he might kill or injure our live sheep or goats.

Moniko opened up a new exit at the back of the kraal. The sheep and goats didn't wait for Moniko to finish moving any stray limbs and twigs. They exploded through the exit to safety and mixed with the cattle.

Now the lion was alone in the sheep kraal with two goat carcasses. The roars were wilder than ever. We could see small bits of red foam on its mouth and freshly painted red paws. I was scared and stood behind Nterere. I trusted his target shooting and was sure his spear would hit its mark and not the earth.

But, to our surprise, the lion stayed where it was.

Some light slowly opened up from the east. It was the sun's rays. Then I saw more than ten warriors Moniko's age. They were from nearby compounds. All with spears. All with swords. There was no doubt; I was sure the lion was going to die.

More light shone from the east. But the lion was not making any move. The warriors tried to provoke the lion into moving by shouting. Then one of the warriors yelled, "STOP! STOP!" He had noticed something unusual.

The lion had no teeth.

Someone said, "No teeth. Must be an old lion then."

Oooh, lucky lion.

It is a dishonor for Maasai warriors to kill lions that are weak, very old, or very young.

My father, Kinki Ole Liaram, joined us and realized it was an old hungry lioness, almost starved, that came to attack our animals. After eating two goats, her belly was too full for her to move around the kraal.

Our home was not far from the park gate. The noise had already reached the rangers. A green Land Rover soon appeared. The rangers took control. The lion was tranquilized. Then they loaded her up to drive her back to the park. They advised my father to go to the park's office to receive cash for the goats killed in the attack.

Some warriors were tense and excited. They wanted to look for strong lions to hunt. The elders spoke to them and finally they calmed down. My father dedicated a lamb to the warriors for their courage.

"Nailang'a," he said in Maa, our tribal language. "A blood milk cocktail will not be amiss on the breakfast menu." And the laughs started.

Nailang'a, a blood milk cocktail, is a Maasai favorite. In Maa, Nailang'a means shiny mixture. It's made from cow's milk plus blood. After a cow's feet are tied to keep it from kicking, a warrior aims an arrow at close range into the cow's neck. The arrow has a disc made from cartilage that stops the point and keeps it from going entirely through the cow's jugular vein and killing it. A woman holding a gourd with milk directs the flow of blood into the gourd. The small wound to the animal's neck is treated, and the cow is released to trot off and join the rest of the herd. The woman whips the blood and milk with a stick till it coagulates and forms a semi-solid drink. I enjoy this drink but, because the blood gives it a slightly salty taste, I prefer to drink plain milk when I herd cattle on hot days.

You may wonder how a lion without teeth could kill the goat, pull it apart, and eat it. It's because a lion has powerful jaws, more powerful than most animals and much more powerful than a human's.

You may also wonder how ten or more Maasai warriors showed up so quickly during the night to help me and Moniko. Remember—this was before cell phones! Maasai families live in houses arranged in a circle. Most are small traditional mud and dung houses and the lion's roar would easily alert even sound sleepers. Some houses are now built of stronger, sturdier materials. This circle of houses, plus an orripie and a kraal (or corral), is called a compound. My village of Oltorotua is made up of eleven of these compounds, all within walking distance of each other.

3

HATARI! DANGER! LION TOO!

My two older brothers, Moniko and Nterere, and I squeezed inside the small orripie. Do you remember I told you an orripie is a small guardhouse? An orripie is built near where the animals stay at night. While two of us slept, the third stood guard in case wandering wildlife thought a cow would be a tasty treat.

With no electricity in the Mara, we lit a branch from an olive tree. Except for that limited light, blackness stretched for miles. Noolamala, our mother, true to the Maasai meaning of her name—"the woman who likes to host"—had cooked an excellent dinner and made creamy chai tea for our family, but the fire she used for cooking had burned out. Now I couldn't see even the short, dark distance across the compound to my house.

Surrounding the houses and kraal was a spiky fence made of acacia tree branches. Thorns 1½ to 2 inches long gave some protection from roaming wildlife, but I knew lions could sneak through the fence. While Moniko and Nterere rested, I took my turn at guard duty.

Suddenly the bells of the oxen started to jingle furiously. I snapped to attention: "Me tuan ena. This cannot be good." I raised the glowing tree branch and saw the cattle were standing. Another sign of danger. Their heads faced in one direction. Very bad.

I had one thought—Hatari! Danger! LION!

Then I heard a lion roar. And another. Two different roars. Both deep and foreboding. I listened and tried to work out how far away the lion was and which direction he was headed. Was he moving toward the kraal or away? Was it two lions? Perhaps a mating pair?

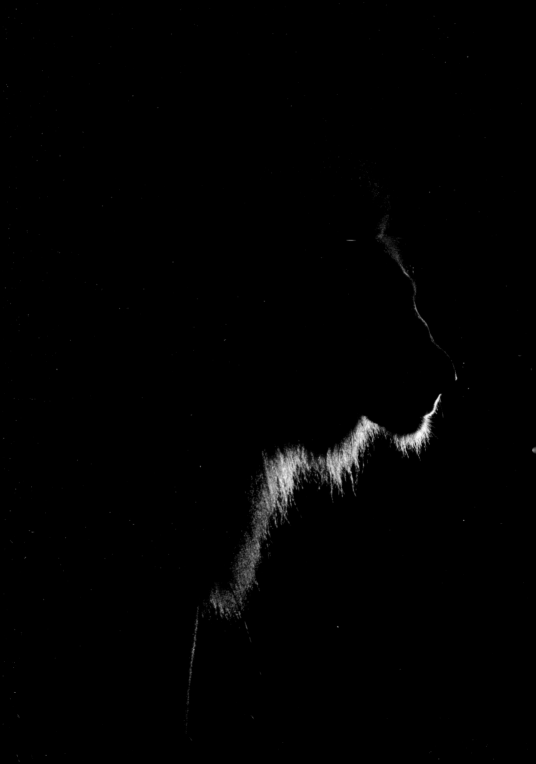

The roars awoke Moniko and Nterere. All three of us grabbed spears, clubs, and bows and arrows. The best weapons in the black night to protect ourselves and the cattle. And also our only weapons.

The cattle heard the lions roar too. The roars spooked them. I knew that frightened cattle try to leap the fence and the spikes can cause serious injury. I whistled loudly. The cattle recognized my special whistle. They knew we were there to protect them.

Moniko, Nterere, and I crept around the outside of the kraal. All three of us yelled. Then we yelled louder. And louder still. As loudly as we could. We hoped to scare the lions and also to get help. Would we come face to face with a large hungry cat? We might, but I knew lions often move on if they sense humans are looking for them.

Warriors from nearby homes ran out and joined the melee. I was relieved. The noisier humans are, the less likely an animal is to attack.

Quiet at last. The lions seemed to have evaporated into the darkness. The cattle were safe.

Neighbors, now eager to hear what happened, joined us. We feared most of all that the lions would return. No, I told them. I believe the lions were probably just passing through on their way to somewhere else. Gradually everyone returned to their houses, but the excitement of the evening and the possibility of the lions coming again kept my brothers and me awake. During the next few nights, extra guards stayed alert in case the lions returned.

They never did.

Losing a cow, whether to a hungry lion or any cause, is painful for a Maasai family. To the Maasai, cattle equal wealth. The common word for cattle is "nkishu," which in Maa, the language of the Maasai, means holders of life. Cows are so central to Maasai life that my father, Kinki Ole Liaram, uses over 100 words to describe cattle, including "iswam," a person's wealth, "inoo-mong'o," providers of food, and "inoopukoret," the family or community feeders.

Although they eat other foods that are easily stored, like cornmeal and dried beans, families depend on cows for milk, especially after Kenya's twice-yearly rainy seasons. Green lush grass to pasture cattle means well-fed cows that give plenty of milk for the family to drink. Including, of course, nailang'a, the milk drink mixed with cow's blood.

The Maasai rely on cows for more than milk. They sleep on cowhides, make shoes, shields, and clothing from their skin, and use fresh urine for cleansing wounds. They also plaster the tree branch walls of their house with dung mixed with soil and water, which loses its smell when baked in the sun. Cattle are so important to Maasai life that they are often gifts for weddings and other events.

4

HATARI! DANGER! RHINOCEROS!

The third day of my guests' stay in the Masai Mara was not the usual sunny sky. It was overcast. We had seen many animals, including four of the "Big 5"—elephant, lion, leopard and Cape buffalo. The only one missing was the elusive rhinoceros.

"The Masai Mara National Reserve is host to about 30 black rhinos. But still, the Mara is so big that it is difficult to spot one," I told my guests.

Experience tells me where to find rhinos. I told my spotter George to be looking near the bushes and along little streams, which rhinos like. These streams are defined by lines of croton bushes. Suddenly, I noticed funny footprints that resembled rhino tracks. I stopped the car and looked down from my window. My guests knew I saw something interesting.

"This is definitely a fresh rhino footprint," I whispered to my guests, who were now excited.

We drove with tortoise speed. We looked inside every bush and down every creek. It was a competition among the guides and guests to see who could spot a rhino first. To our anxious eyes, every tree shadow or termite mound looked like one.

George saw an animal two miles ahead. It looked like a buffalo but slightly smaller. As he pointed it out to me, I counted this as one lucky day in the Mara. A black rhino is very difficult to spot.

I directed my Land cruiser toward the animal. As we drove closer, the actual animal was what we hoped.

All the guests whispered, "Wow! Wow! Rhinoceros!"

It was the second time that month for me to have spotted a rhino. I was so excited, I forgot to tell my guests to maintain silence. Rhinos don't like noise. "Black rhinos are very aggressive and shy," I told my guests. "They have very good hearing but poor eyesight."

The rhino was now about 200 yards away. Guests with big camera lenses could get very clear photos. Those with baby cameras spoke to themselves. "Bluuurry."

The rhino was becoming restless. I told my guests to keep quiet. I tried to circle around the rhino for a better view. The grass was high, about one meter above the ground.

As I drove further round the bush, the rhino seemed to be following us and coming closer. Definitely a big male!

Then we saw a female rhino with a young calf hiding in the bush. The male was probably coming to meet them. Did he think we would harm his family?

Suddenly, a splash of falling leaves erupted from the bush. In my driver's mirror, I could see a charging animal.

Fffffff! Fffff! The animal was making noise.

"Staaay calm" I whispered to my guests. With a charging rhino, driving fast will make the situation worse. I stopped the car. Everyone was frozen and attached to his or her seat. My foot was shaking on the gear pedal!

Now not normal safari excitement. NOW—Hatari! Danger! RHINO!

The rhino didn't stop. He stabbed my spare tire two times with his sharp horn. Our Land cruiser shook. We shook. Hsssssssssssh! The exploding tire pressure produced a loud sound.

Hatari! Rhinoceros!

This was the most hatari I had ever witnessed in my career as a safari guide. My heart was beating fast. An interesting sighting—but very dangerous and frightening to my guests.

No guest had the courage to take more photos.

In a minute, the baby rhino in the bush ran away in the opposite direction. For a female rhino, staying close to a calf is more important than charging unknown objects like vehicles. The mother rhino hurriedly followed the calf. The male rhino must have sensed no more danger from us, but I did not move the vehicle until he was out of sight.

It took a while before everyone regained the energy to talk about the hatari incident. Only one guest captured a photo of the charging rhino—and it was blurry. Everyone else had photos only of the big male when we first saw him.

The guests commented that the rhino charge was the highlight of their safari experience. "Now we feel that we are in the heart of true African wilderness with dangerous animals around us," said one. Another said, "No doubt about it—African animals are dangerous."

After my anxiety subsided, I turned around to my guests and reminded them, "All animals in the African wilderness are certainly dangerous. Especially if the animal feels agitated, frightened, or threatened by anyone. One needs to be careful with all animals, including small antelopes. They can all be dangerous. Very hatari!"

Everyone listened keenly. Then we headed toward a beautiful flattop acacia tree where we knew we could safely set up our picnic lunch. As we enjoyed our meal in the middle of the Masai Mara, everyone could not stop talking about how he or she had felt when the rhino charged.

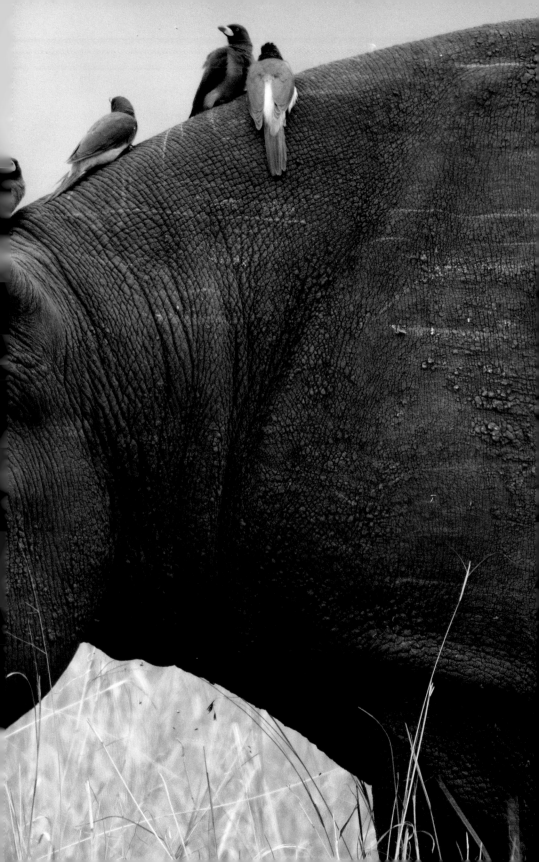

BUT WAIT! THERE'S MORE...

White Rhino

Black Rhino

Although they are huge animals, rhinos eat only vegetation and are not predators who feed on other animals. There are two species of rhino in Africa: Black and White. The black rhino is not black and the white rhino is not white. They are both grey. How did they get the names? Not because of their color but because of their faces.

The white rhino has a wide mouth or snout. The name wide may have been mispronounced as white and the name stuck. The black, which has a hooked lip mouth, then became the opposite of the white.

Because of the shapes of their mouths, black and white rhinos have different eating habits and live in different areas. Black rhino are browsers that like staying in bushes, not open areas. White rhinos are grazers so they prefer open areas.

Both white and black rhino horns are made of keratin, the same material in our fingernails. It is not ivory. Keratin is compressed hair.

There are two main reasons rhinos are near extinction. First, humans are moving onto lands where the rhinos live. Second, they are hunted for their horns. The horns are prized in Asia because of false beliefs about the medical power of their horns when ground into a powder and eaten.

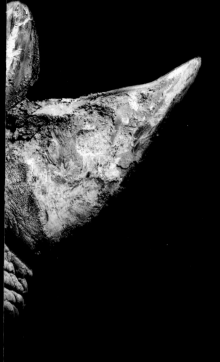

There are two subspecies of the white rhino: northern and southern. Sadly, as of 2021, there are only two northern white rhinos left in the world. Both females, they live in Olpejeta Conservancy in Kenya. There are about 20,000 southern white rhinos. With only about 5,500 black rhinos left in the wild in Africa, they now are also an endangered species.

5

HATARI! DANGER! BUFFALO!

Each day my visitors take three game drives. If you go with us, you enjoy a great view from the safety of my 4-wheel drive vehicle while you watch wildlife roam freely across the Masai Mara. With this schedule, you have a good chance to see different animals and birds before breakfast, at midday, and in early evening.

On our morning game drive, you may see giraffes, zebras, hyenas, and a lioness with cubs. Then at midday, perhaps wildebeests, ostriches, and elephants march before your eyes.

As the day cools, you watch a herd of African buffalo leisurely graze on golden grasses that stretch for miles. I point out the birds on the back of a huge buffalo. "See the little birds on the buffalo's back? They are along for the ride. They are also along for dinner. These birds pick off bugs that live on the animal's tough hide."

You might ask how else buffalo spend their days. Well, they lick a termite mound for salt, nap in the hot afternoon sun, and stop at a watering hole for a drink. As

you watch them meander across the Mara plain, strolling leisurely along, buffalo seem to live an easy, relaxed life.

Many villages are in the same areas where buffalo herds roam. I remember outrunning buffalo. I was most probably one of the youngest kids walking to school in our village, but I was one of the best runners. I can flash back and see myself running in front of very huge bulls. I am smart enough not to do that now. African buffalo are responsible for about 200 human deaths a year. HATARI! DANGER!

A buffalo charge is often deadly because the buffalo doing the charging, he is very cunning. I say he because it is almost always an old male buffalo that tends to wander alone or perhaps in a small group. He hears and smells much better than we do and, long before we spot him, he senses we bring danger. So he hides under some cover, like tall grass, and quietly waits for us to get closer. And closer. And closer. And then—charge. He rushes recklessly, with alarming speed. And once he begins a charge, he doesn't stop. This beast runs and hurls his massive body toward his target. Then he slashes with his thick curved horns and kicks with his hooves.

His surprise attack and swiftness make it difficult to get out of the way or climb a tree. Someone with a gun may not have time to take careful aim. Buffalo run so fast when they charge that many hunters can only shoot at the

buffalo's footsteps. Even a rifle bullet that hits where the horns join may not pierce the buffalo's head, his hide is so tough. Few humans live to tell how they escaped from an angry buffalo.

I am one of the lucky ones. I was with two friends when a buffalo charged us. We escaped by climbing a tree. But the buffalo stayed below for two hours. He walked around and around the tree while waiting for us to come down. I know people who were forced to stay in trees for many hours, but two hours was long enough. We clung onto the branches of the tree. He looked up at us and snorted—a sign that the buffalo was charged up and ready to charge. It was hard to tell the difference between the wind shaking the tree and our bodies shaking. The tree was trembling from a combination of both.

You may hear the story that buffalo urinate on their tails. When they flick their tail, the urine flies up into the air. If it lands on you, it makes you itch and scratch until you fall out of the tree. This is a belief among many people. I take it as fiction. I don't believe that a buffalo can understand that urine causes itching. That would be a very clever buffalo.

Even if they are not quite that clever, visitors should beware. Stay in your vehicle when on safari in Africa.

Don't Be Buffaloed by These Facts

Along with elephants, lions, leopards, and rhinos, buffalo are one of the "Big Five," the five most dangerous animals in Africa. A healthy male weighs up to 1800 pounds.

African buffalo are also known as Cape Buffalo.

No one knows for sure why buffalo become angry and charge. Perhaps a lone bull buffalo or those in a small herd may not feel safe. Since they see only in black and white, a buffalo may fear anything that is upright, as humans are.

Some Africans call them "widow-makers" and, because the hide of a male buffalo is very dark, they are also called "black death."

Calves have red coats. The coats of females stay reddish, but males' coats turn very dark, brown or black.

Females live in a large herd with calves and breeding males. The herd provides safety from lions and other predators.

Baby calves stay hidden in grasses until they are a few weeks old. Then they travel in the center of the herd for protection.

rsabit

African Buffalo

Wallowing in mud helps a buffalo get rid of ticks and other parasites and keeps its skin healthy.

Other animals seldom prey on buffaloes because of their size and horns. One buffalo can kill a lion, but usually several lions are needed to kill a buffalo. Even the fierce croc skips a meal of buffalo unless it spies a young calf or one that is old and weak.

Water buffalo, which live primarily in Asia, can be domesticated and trained to work for humans. They are a different species from African buffalo. Also completely different are what some people call American or European buffalo, which are actually a separate animal known as bison.

Water Buffalo

Bison

6

HATARI! DANGER! ELEPHANT!

When I was quite a young boy, I found it fun walking to school very early in the morning. We were about 20 of us from the nearby compounds. Every day we were supposed to start classes at eight in the morning but sometimes wild animals, like elephants and buffalo, got in the way. Then our parents would not allow us to leave the village. We'd be forced to stay home for a long time. When the wild animals passed, we could get on our way to school.

Now I like to see animals close by when I take visitors on safari. Most trips are by jeep or van, but some are nature walks near our safari camp.

One day, the sun promised it would soon be sizzling hot, but the morning sky was a jewel blue. I led a group of about eight visitors on a walk between two small hills. As we walked, I pointed out plants. "This is aloe," I told them. "Aloe is very good for the skin. But never taste it. It's very bitter."

David, a guard who carried a gun, was with us. Killing wild animals is not allowed in Kenya. A guard uses a gun only to save a human life. Our job is to protect wildlife and leave the land exactly as we find it.

A small herd of elephants was about a half-mile away, a good distance. As I talked, I sensed the mother elephant looking toward us. I trained my eyes on her. All at once, her huge ears spread wide, funneling sound, the way a person cups a hand around an ear to hear better. Her ears told me she was fearful and wanted to protect her baby.

I turned to face the group. I spoke quietly but with a firm voice: "Stay calm and don't move, but, if I give a command, do as I tell you."

I whispered to David, "Move to the side the elephant will come from if she charges."

Suddenly, leaving her baby and sounding a deep trumpet, she began a charge over the grassland that separated her herd from us humans.

Hatari! Danger! ELEPHANT!

David moved to be in position if he were forced to shoot. The rest of us froze.

The elephant stopped but she seemed nervous. She lifted her trunk and looked around. She was still about a quarter-mile away. That is about the length of three soccer fields—as you call our game of football. But I knew

a rampaging elephant can travel quickly over bare land. If she charged again she could reach us fast.

I was afraid our scent would tell the elephant where we were. I saw an acacia tree nearby. A small tree is no protection against the world's biggest land animal, but it might help hide our scent.

"Everyone follow me," I quietly said. "We need to move away from the direction of the wind so the elephant can't smell us."

David also moved around behind the small tree to make sure the elephant did not catch his scent.

We held our breath and waited.

And waited.

And waited.

The elephant still seemed edgy and upset. Would she again charge toward us?

Hapana. No.

Probably because she could not smell or see anything, the elephant returned to the herd.

We continued our walk toward camp. The visitors were anxious to share their adventure with others over lunch. Great fun and laughs now.

I also relaxed. I told my guests, "Ahh, turn around and you can see the mother elephant suckle her calf."

BUT WAIT! THERE'S MORE...

Five Facts About Elephants

African elephants are larger than Asian elephants and have large ears shaped much like a map of Africa.

A newborn African elephant weighs about 220 pounds. A full-grown male can weigh as much as 13,000 pounds. In other words, this largest land animal on earth weighs over twice as much as a big van.

An elephant is too heavy to jump or run but can move across a field at 15 miles per hour.

Poaching for elephant tusks has put elephants on the vulnerable list—in danger of becoming extinct. But tusks are much like bone and have no special qualities.

The skin of elephants takes on the color of the mud in which they love to roll.

7

HATARI! DANGER! CROCODILE!

The Great Migration is a wonder of nature. Hundreds of thousands of wildebeests, joined by zebras and several kinds of antelope, begin the long trek between Kenya's Masai Mara and neighboring Tanzania's vast plain, the Serengeti. Many generations of these animals have made this trip. The trip is dangerous for them because they are prey for predators, for animals that hunt them for food.

"Why do they make this trip?" you ask.

No one can answer for sure, but the Great Migration begins each year with dry weather. Lack of rain means less grass for these plant-eating animals. To reach fresh lush green grass, their dangerous trip includes swimming across the Mara River.

The first arrivals in the Mara usually come in June. They congregate and roam the area near the river. Finally, a few risk their lives by jumping into the water. Others follow, and then still others. With long, swishing tails and blowing beards, the wildebeests and their partners in travel explode into a thudding, thumping mass and frantically jump into the water.

My guests had come especially to experience the Great Migration and were very excited. We started the day early with a picnic breakfast and packed our lunch into the car. Although guests usually love to watch the Big Cats for a long time, today our stop to see lions and leopards was only a minute.

Ten minutes after entering the gate to the Mara Reserve, my guests knew what Great Migration means. As far as they could see, thousands of wildebeests seemed to be spread all over the Mara plains.

As we drove closer, we saw they were formed into lines of stampede, moving toward the Mara River. Enkipai is the proper name for the Mara River in Maa, meaning bright flowing water. This perfectly describes the waters of the Mara.

Every safari guide drives alongside the herds. As I wiggled my car in line, I told my guests, "This crossing looks promising."

After not too long, thousands of animals congregated on the bank of the river. "Mooo. Mooo. Moooo" filled the air.

Along with the other safari guides, I parked my vehicle at least 328 feet, or less than 1/4 mile, from the river crossing. This is to give respect to the animals and it is a general rule in the Mara.

From my experience, animal pressure building up from all sides means a crossing is about to happen. I advised my guests to have their cameras ready.

Shortly, a cloud of dust twisted over the wildebeests. "Crossing, crossing," everyone shouted. Several vehicle engines squeaked at once, followed by a quick drive toward the crossing point.

Having been a guide for many years, I parked my vehicle to the side and not in the middle of the cluster of vehicles. I wanted to have access to smooth driving when the crossing began. I parked right at an angle facing the center of the crossing line. Because my vehicle had an open roof, visitors viewed from above and from both sides.

My guests watched in wonder as hundreds of animals splashed like thunder in the swollen river. The cheers of excited tourists were heard from all over.

"Please maintain silence," I said to my guests. Maintaining silence is part of respecting the wildlife and other tourists and guides.

My guests paid attention and honored my instructions. I could hear only the bings of video cameras and photo shutters....crrrrrr, crrrr, chhhr, chhhhr.

Several crocodiles waited on the sandy bank above the water. Suddenly, a huge mamba (Swahili for crocodile) swam toward the crossing wildebeests.

"Croc."

It was like a moving log, mouth wide open and teeth ready to bite anything. Several zebra quickly jumped past the croc's gaping mouth.

The croc submerged itself in the water and we missed where it went. From the middle of the crossing wildebeests, we heard the cry of a struggling one. It was a baby and the crocodile dragged it downstream while its mother stood helplessly by. Splashes of blood painted the water and the shouts of sympathetic tourists were heard. Ooooh-no. Crocodile, stop.

Hatari! Danger! CROCODILE!

The crocodile pulled the wildebeest to the deepest part of the river. The tail of the croc was seen propelled in the water and chains of teeth locked into the wildebeest body. Hatari!

Several other crocodiles, mostly small ones, bit the poor wildebeest steak from all sides.

With some crocs eating, this was a good chance for other wildebeests to have a safer crossing. More and more wildebeests jumped down the bank and over the heads of others in their stampede across the river. Zebras and some antelopes also took advantage of this safe time to cross the Mara.

But one wildebeest is not enough to feed more than five crocodiles. Another massive croc appeared, ready to attack. This one was fast moving. The wildebeests were already aware of the first attack on their colleague.

The sound of the roaring river mixed with the sound of the animals as they raced to reach the other side. As a visitor, at this time you can either choose to watch a lively crossing or watch crocodiles pulling wildebeests into river butchery.

For about an hour, most of my visitors watched the wildebeests jumping down the bank. Then the tension built up. My guests wanted to again see the hungry crocs fill their stomachs. They got right to the point. "It is a safe crossing. Where are the crocodiles?"

Suddenly crocodiles appeared.

Perhaps an experienced wildebeest noticed the coming of a crocodile, as it suddenly turned around. Others followed.

Many wildebeests moved along the river in search of another crossing. Most often some will come back to cross at the same place. Or if it is close to dark, they will wait near the river till the next day. They don't cross on dark nights but, on some occasions, crossings have been seen during moonlit nights.

My guests chattered on the way back to camp about all they had to tell friends at home and the photos they would show them.

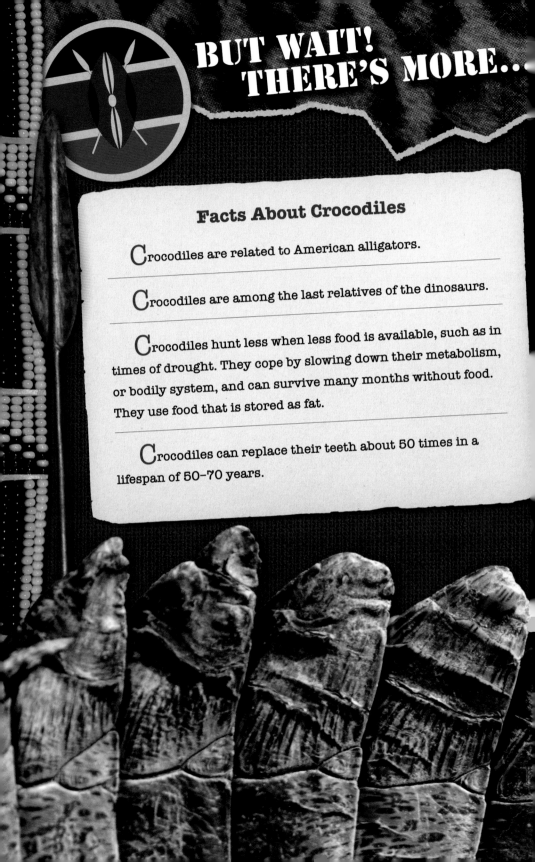

BUT WAIT! THERE'S MORE...

Facts About Crocodiles

Crocodiles are related to American alligators.

Crocodiles are among the last relatives of the dinosaurs.

Crocodiles hunt less when less food is available, such as in times of drought. They cope by slowing down their metabolism, or bodily system, and can survive many months without food. They use food that is stored as fat.

Crocodiles can replace their teeth about 50 times in a lifespan of 50–70 years.

Kaprosuchus was a carnivorous crocodile that lived in Niger, Africa during the Cretaceous Period.

Crocodile

American Alligator

8

HATARI! DANGER! THREE LIONS!

In my last chapter, I told you about the Great Migration of wildebeests, joined by some zebras and antelopes. At the same time, there is another Great Migration. Each year, between June and October, millions of visitors from around the world migrate to Kenya and Tanzania to view the migrating animals.

I was driving four guests in my open-sided four-by-four vehicle one hot day. We were headed for the Mara River because we knew the Great Migration had begun. My spotter Teketi sat on my left. Both of us watched for wildlife on our way to the river, and with Teketi's help I could also pay attention to the bumps in the road.

As we neared the Mara River we saw the Great Migration in full view. Many huge animals were plunging into the mighty Mara, swimming across, and struggling to climb the bank on the other side.

Wildebeest and zebras are not the only animals we saw. Hungry crocodiles waited in the Mara River's water and along the banks. They were ready to make fresh kills.

Then we spotted four young male lions. Hatari! SIMBA. Danger! LION.

My guests often tell me a lion is the animal they want most to see. They have seen the lion, or simba in Swahili, in zoos and movies. Now they hope to see him roaming wild on the plains of his home. What great luck to see four waiting in the bushes along the river!

One of the lions quickly jumped into the swollen river and grabbed a wildebeest. The poor wildebeest tried to swim back into the river but the lion was too strong and pulled him toward shore.

Two other lions joined the hunt. The three of them grabbed the wildebeest from the water above the rocky bank. They squeezed his neck and strangled the wildebeest to death and then started feasting on the animal's carcass. While they ate, they seemed to talk to each other. We could hear roars and see sharp teeth like needles painted red with blood.

Such is the way of nature. For human guests to the Mara, rule #1 is: Watch; do not interfere.

So we watched. The lions ate for an hour. We could see their bellies were swollen.

The hot sun was now scorching. The lions needed some shade. My vehicle was parked between the lions and the croton bushes. Because croton bushes are one of a lion's favorite hiding places, I thought they would rest there. But the lions decided to find shade under our vehicle. One by one, all three crept under our open-sided jeep. Directly under our feet.

Hatari! Danger! LION.

Could we be the ones in danger?

We soon could hear heavy breathing and deep snoring under our feet. Other tourists enjoyed taking photos of us and the lions below our jeep. My guests, however, were nervous. I told them we had nothing to worry about. I knew the lions had full bellies and so were not dangerous.

Another Mara rule is that animals have the absolute right to do as they wish in the Mara. Tourists and guides have to respect animals and treat them with care. I therefore knew I should not disturb the lions under us. Turning on the jeep's engine while they lay under it would have disturbed them. The engine noise would also have disturbed the other guests and guides watching our little story unfolding.

My guests could only peep out of the jeep. They couldn't see much of the snoozing lions below them. They saw tuft of tails and whiskers being blown by wind.

It was noon. The sun was high in the sky. We waited.

We waited.

And waited.

How long would the lions nap?

Still no movement. We wondered when the lions would wake up and wander on.

Three hours passed. The lions slept quietly. My guests seriously needed lunch. Though it was hot, the guests were more focused on their fear of the lions than the heat. The ladies had to hold off "checking the tire pressure," as we say here in the Mara. You might say going to the restroom. One of the men filled an empty water bottle.

Then Teketi said he had an idea. "Look at this," he said. "Let's make some artificial rain to wake up the lions."

Teketi made a hole on the cap of a bottle of water.

Hiding under the canvas, he sprayed water through an open window onto the lions' tails and manes. The lions didn't hear thunder...but they felt rain.

Slowly the lions crept out of the vehicle's shadow. They shook the water off their manes. Sprays of water filled the air.

I slowly pulled the jeep back, away from the lions. As I drove away, I could hear deep breaths from my guests behind me. I also heard various sounds of relief and happiness. "Wow...Oooh...Haaah...Finally...I'm starving."

The next voice I heard behind me said, "Lunch."

We watched the lions shake the water from their manes as I pulled away. I drove straight to a famous picnic site overlooking the Mara River. My guests ate and watched the river, still filled with hippos and crocodiles.

As we enjoyed our lunch, several of my guests could not stop talking about how close the lions were, while others still felt fear and said only, "STOP! Enough please."

BUT WAIT! THERE'S MORE...

The Mara is the place to witness the Great Migration. And also to have encounters with the big cats of Africa.

One hundred years ago, the African lion population was estimated to be over 200,000. Now their numbers are down to only about 20,000 and the areas in which lions roam is much smaller.

Africa Geographic named the Serengeti-Mara area as the prime location to see this king of beasts. Their website says, "...the wide-open savannah plains of the Masai Mara National Reserve make for excellent lion viewing of large prides that are accustomed to tourist vehicles. The Mara lions have been made famous by the popular BBC TV series, Big Cat Diaries."

9

HATARI! DANGER! OSTRICH!

My guests and I like to watch ostriches as they prance across the Mara. These huge, stately African birds are very strong. They don't fly but, because of their long legs, they are fast runners. In fact, they can compete with a cheetah. Or with a car going 60 miles per hour.

Guests also enjoy watching hyenas. Like pet cats, hyenas groom themselves and leave their scent. However, they look more like dogs. They have well-padded feet, with claws that let them grip the ground, so they are good runners and can make sharp turns.

While driving my guests in the Mara one morning, I saw a hyena walking aimlessly around in the bush. I knew the hyena was looking for a morning meal. I also knew hyenas, like many of us, love eggs for breakfast.

They especially like ostrich eggs. Right away, I sensed something was about to happen and my guests would see the excitement.

Sure enough—the hyena bumped into an ostrich nest hidden in the long grass. What a find! Nearly 20 eggs were in the clutch. You may use the word clutch to mean grabbing onto something. Or you might say a player in a tight game got nervous in the clutch. But clutch is also a word that means the eggs a bird has laid in a nest.

This clutch meant many omelets for the hyena. He smashed four eggs and gobbled down the sac fluid and crushed yolk. The odor of broken eggs filled the air.

Since both male and female ostriches take turns sitting on a nest, the male ostrich was close by and smelled the odor of the broken eggs.

The feet of the ostrich moved so fast that they didn't seem to touch the ground. He stepped into the grassy nest. The hyena screamed with fear and dashed away. First the ostrich had to confirm the damage to the eggs and for sure he did. Four eggs were crushed and others had rolled away and lay on the bare ground.

The hyena screamed even before the ostrich moved toward him.

Then the chase started. Ostrich versus hyena. Long legs versus short legs.

I turned my vehicle around. My guests cheered. I drove fast beside the chase. We bumped across the Mara, trying to keep up. Ostrich moved even faster than vehicle.

After a few hundred yards, the ostrich caught the hyena.

Kick 1.

Kick 2.

Ostrich mouth open and wings raised high.

Kick 3.

Kick 4.

The ostrich was not going to let the hyena get away. Hyena screams filled the savannah.

We watched. In the Mara the rule is to watch nature unfold. Not to interfere.

Only ten kicks and the hyena was dead.

Hatari! Danger! MBUNI! OSTRICH!

Some of my guests cheered with joy. They felt as if they were watching a nature movie. Some had hoped to see tiny ostrich embryos and were disappointed to see only yolk in the eggs. Others pitied the hyena.

We watched as the ostrich walked back to the nest. He assembled the rolled eggs together and sat on them. He made a croaking noise. Was he crying about the broken eggs?

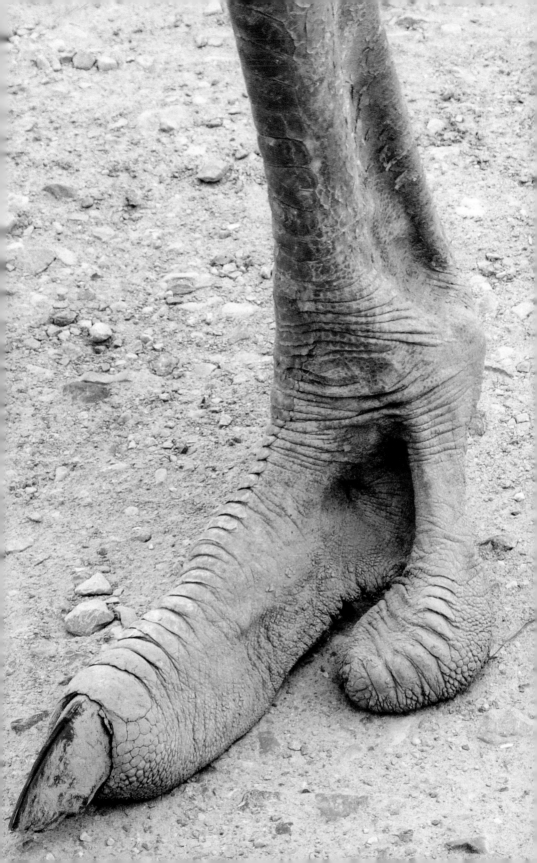

Spotted Hyena

Striped Hyena

ostrich egg with
chicken egg

Male ostrich

Female ostrich

Facts About Ostriches and Hyenas

A male ostrich makes a booming sound, similar to a lion's roar. It is the Maasai's traditional sign of coming rain. Female ostriches can only hiss.

There are two types of ostriches. One is the Masai or Common Ostrich and the other is the Somali Ostrich. The difference is the color of breeding males. Common Ostrich males have pink legs and necks, whereas Somali Ostrich males have blue legs and necks.

You can easily tell a Masai male ostrich from a female. The male has black and white feathers. The female is brown.

A hyena can easily bite into an ostrich egg.

Hyena babies are born with sharp teeth. They can bite soon after birth.

We have both Spotted and Striped hyenas in the Mara. Striped are very rare and are nocturnal.

Hyenas kill more Maasai livestock than lions, leopards, and cheetahs combined. I think of them as the opportunists of the African savannah because they take food that is easily found.

10

HATARI! DANGER! LEOPARD VERSUS HYENA!

The only light in the Mara at night comes from the moon and stars. My guests on an early morning game drive were astonished with my navigation skills when we started driving around while it was still mostly dark.

Soon dawn's light broke. Enasirie. This means "as the rays spark the horizon." This is when the streams of early light fill the sky above the rising sun. A perfect sunrise.

The bawls of wildebeest filled the air. All around us, we saw wildebeest wandering. During the dark night, a huge herd of these odd-looking antelopes had been separated on the plains of the Masai Mara. There, many predators lay in wait for easy prey like a wildebeest.

A predator is an animal that hunts or kills other

animals for food. The animal a predator kills is called the prey. Visitors to the Mara never know if they will see an animal as prey or as predator. That is both the joy and the hard truth of watching nature in action.

The wildebeest wanted to keep their herds intact, not lose a member to a predator, and so they gave us a beautiful show by running in lines all around us.

Have you ever seen a wildebeest? The stripes on a zebra inspire awe. The lion has his elegant mane. The elephant is huge—over 8000 pounds! But to me a wildebeest looks sort of silly, like three animals combined—buffalo head, cow body, and horse tail.

Before not too long, I noticed the curious behavior of some wildebeest. Perhaps they could smell a predator. Nervous antelopes always tell the guides in the Mara that a cat is around.

Soompe Ronko, my spotter, and I looked around the bushes.

Soompe shouted, "Caaat, cat!" Everyone in my van turned around but didn't know where to look.

"Where? Where?" I asked.

"Next to you," Soompe said.

A leopard was just 20 meters from our car. That's about the distance from home plate to the pitcher's mound on a baseball field.

"Wow!" my guests whispered.

The leopard was on the move, stalking through the

grass and bushes. There was no point in telling my guests the leopard was hunting. Everyone could see that.

We all looked around to see the leopard's prey. I saw a grazing calf wildebeest 50 meters behind the bushes. I whispered to my guests, "Please direct your cameras to the wildebeest. The leopard is going to sprint fast."

Before the last word was out of my mouth, a cloud of dust was around the wildebeest. The rest of the wildebeests ran around in panic and curiosity. Fffff! Fffff! Ffff! Snouts all around the place.

Screams from a suffocating calf pained our nerves.

Grrrrhh! Grrrrhh! Grrrh! The calf cried.

Hatari! Danger! LEOPARD!

The leopard pushed his teeth into the throat of the wildebeest to suffocate him.

Chui in Swahili. Olkinya lasho in Maa. In English: calf eater!

I drove much closer to the leopard and the dying wildebeest calf for my guests to get better photographs. The guests seemed to feel one of three ways: "I have the courage to take good photos" or "Ugh! I don't like staring at the wildebeest" or "I pity the wildebeest."

Finally the wildebeest seemed dead and the leopard started eating its fresh breakfast.

Bite one.

Bite two.

The wildebeest again screamed. The scream was loud. Very loud. The scream scared the leopard—the wildebeest was supposed to be dead.

The wildebeest's cry pierced the quiet of the Mara and echoed far across the savannah. It was so loud that it attracted other predators, like hyenas.

One hyena appeared out of nowhere...and another one...and another one. Several jackals also joined the escort leading to the action.

Within a short while, a large number of hyenas had gathered around the leopard. They snatched the leopard's food with the force of their bites. The poor leopard had no choice but to quit. He climbed up an acacia tree.

A dozen hyenas ferociously fought over the meal with laughs and screams of triumph.

The poor leopard looked down from above, his tail hanging on the tree's forked branch.

More than six jackals also did not miss the party. They surrounded the hyenas and collected pieces of flesh and licked drops of blood that fell on the ground.

Above our heads, we saw shadows of vultures and eagles flying in the sky before they landed to do the final cleansing of the site.

Nature is amazing! Nothing is wasted! Even the last drop of blood is food for someone.

BUT WAIT! THERE'S MORE...

Facts About Leopards, Wildebeests, Jackals, and Vultures, Plus a Few More About Hyenas

Wildebeests, a type of antelope, are also known as gnus—pronounced noo to rhyme with a cow's moo.

Leopards are difficult to see on safari. Their elusiveness, courage, and tough hunting skills have earned them a place on the African big five.

Leopards are the closest relatives of lions. They are in the Genus Panthera.

Hyenas don't only scavenge food. A hyena is strong enough to fight a leopard and steal its kill.

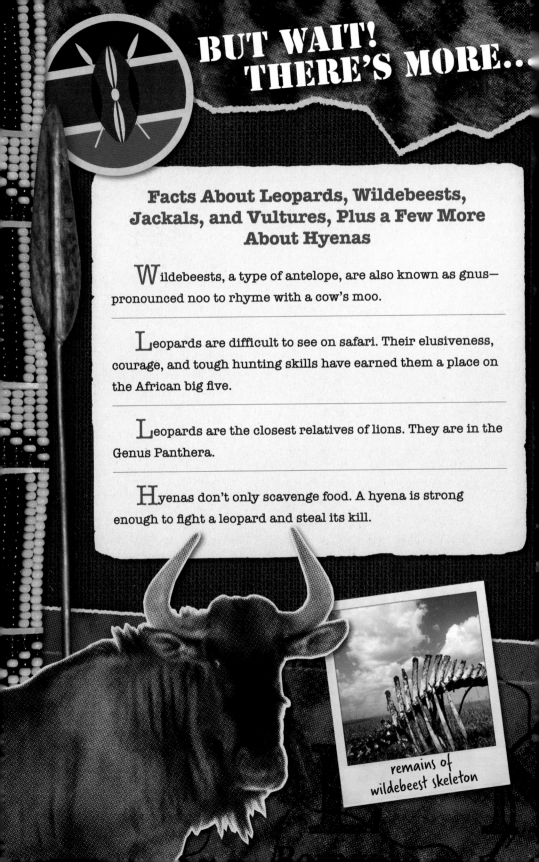

remains of wildebeest skeleton

Hyenas are the second-most successful African predator after the lion. The leopard is third and the cheetah fourth.

Both hyenas and jackals are called carnivores because they eat meat; however, they don't eat each other—they are friends while scavenging food in the savannah.

The hyena is a different animal from the jackal, although they look similar from a distance. Hyenas are larger, with taller front limbs than hind limbs.

Vultures are an important bird because they do the most cleanup at the sites of kills.

Jackal

Hyena

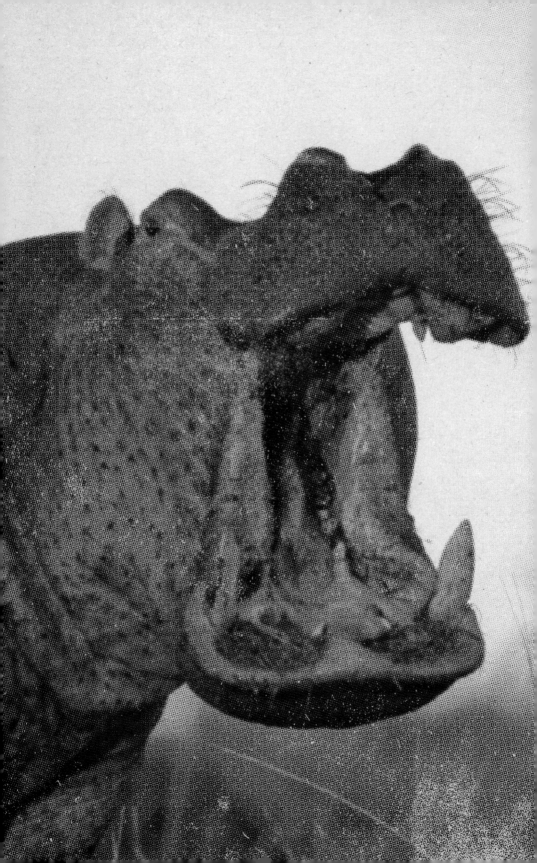

11

HATARI! DANGER! HIPPO!

Never get between a hippo and a pool of water. Hatari sana! Very dangerous!

Here is a story I often tell my guests to the Mara.

My father, Kinki Ole Liaram, was herding cattle along the Mara River. The cattle took turns as they carefully made their way down the bank of the river for a drink.

Suddenly Kinki heard bells. Bells from around the necks of his steers. The bells told my father something was wrong.

He walked fast along the bank to inspect. He hoped to see a familiar lion mane. We Maasai often encounter lions. We are forbidden to kill them but we have experience and know how to deal with them.

Good or bad, he knew this was not a lion. Something different was scaring the cattle.

Then he saw a charging hippo. Baby Hippo followed behind. Not what he expected. An unusual thing to see.

Kinki knew hippos are one of the largest land animals and a female weighs as much as a small car. Being run over by a car—not good. But because she is built like a big, squatty barrel, fast turns while running are not possible for a hippo—unlike a man.

Kinki was also aware a hippo feels threatened if trapped in the middle of cattle. Reactions from other animals makes it more aggressive. Any animal that has free space will relax and be less violent.

Kinki quickly thought what to do. He ran down to the water and then turned back along the sandy bank.

The hippo did, too, and the chase began....

Could Kinki jump in the river to take the hippo's attention away from the herd?

NO. He saw bubbles from hungry crocodiles. Not the right time to swim.

The hippo bellowed loudly. She splashed brown water as she chased him.

Kinki moved up the bank and saw a small trench that water had worn away. A small narrow gap in the trench might save him. It fit only a man, not a fat hippo.

The hippo bellowed along the sandy bank.

As Kinki crept into the gap he saw the hippo shaking her head. He heard her roaring. The angry hippo wanted to get him out of the gully. She splashed dung on him.

No problem. A shower of hippo dung was better than a crushing bite with her huge teeth.

Then Kinki saw the baby hippo stuck in the bank's mud. The mother hippo saw too and turned away from Kinki. Not important anymore to chase the man. She had to push her baby out of the mud.

"Hatari sana!" my father said and used the shuka he wore as a cape to wipe away sweat.

Our family's cattle grazed fearlessly on lush pasture along the banks of the river as my father watched the hippo and calf swim downstream. "Most lucky day," he said to himself.

Ooh, watch out. Never be between a hippo and a pool of water—then you will be safe.

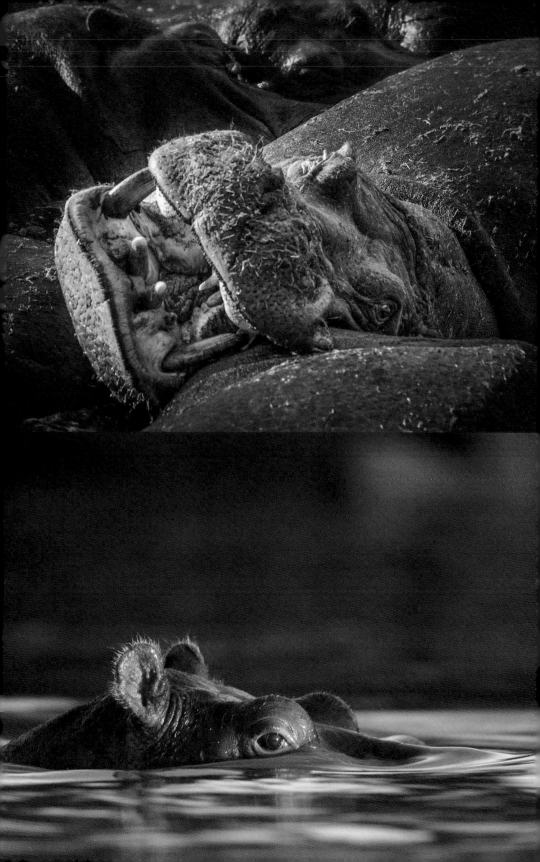

Know These Hippo Facts

Hippos are aggressive and territorial. These traits have long made them one of the most feared animals in Africa, even by those who live around wildlife. If you're crossing a stream on foot, you can easily mistake the back of a hippo for a rock.

Hippos eat mostly grasses— about 132 pounds (60 kilograms) every day—so they are not a known threat to cattle.

Hippopotamus is Greek for River Horse but they are not scientifically related to horses; their closest relatives are pigs, whales, and dolphins.

The hippo is at risk, or "vulnerable," for extinction. Hippos face disease and drought and lose habitat when people claim land near water for their own use.

Although hippos don't swim, they spend about 16 hours each day in water to keep their skin cool and moist. They can see, breathe, and hear while underwater because their eyes, nose, and ears are on top of their heads.

When out of water, hippos have glands that produce a red liquid to protect their almost hairless skin from sun. This liquid is not sweat.

Female hippos are usually more sweet-tempered than males, but not if their baby is threatened.

When male hippos defecate, they tend to twirl their tails. As the tail twirls, poop is slung from their body in an arc.

12

HATARI! DANGER! WHAT IS IT?

If you stay in a camp in the Masai Mara, you may enjoy a fancy dinner in an outdoor tent. Our weather is mild and perfect for informal meals. When you finish and step outside the tent, you might hear a horrible sound coming from trees.

The sound is like a clacker noisemaker. Or maybe a huge metal gate as its parts grind against each other when it's opened. Quick, where is the camp guard? The noise seems to come from a huge animal.

Hatari! Danger!—WHAT IS IT?

Each day before our morning safari, I meet my guests and ask how their night was. Most report that in the evening and very early morning they heard scary sounds from a large and loud animal that lives in the trees.

Everyone then asks, "What was that? Was it a hyena?" Some reply no, not a hyena, the sound is too loud. Must be something big. Maybe a hippo.

Conversations like this happened often. I never knew what to tell them.

My colleagues and I spent a lot of time asking ourselves, "What big animal sounds that loud at our camp?" We were very puzzled.

One night, I decided to stay awake to hear for myself. I stayed up till past midnight. I could hear only small animals like hyraxes and bush babies. I gave up and went to bed. I was too bored to listen more.

I decided to wake up early. It was the time of the morning star—Kileken to us Maasai. I took wake-up tea to one of my guests. He was so happy to hear my voice. "Jackson! Jackson!" he shouted. "What is making the big screams? Scary!"

Hatari! I held my head down to listen. All I heard were hyraxes calling from every tree.

"Jackson, come inside! It is coming closer!" the guest shouted.

Then we both heard a noise like several blacksmiths hammering their metal. Yes, the sound was deafening.

Ooooh, now I knew. Right above the tent, a series of croaking hyrax screams exploded. The noise was from this small, harmless animal about as big as a rabbit. I had lived with their noise all my life, but my guests thought their lives were in danger.

150

"Hakuna hatari! No danger!" I said to my guest.

I grasped my torch and shined it on the tree. A small animal was screaming. Sounds hatari—but is not hatari.

BUT WAIT! THERE'S MORE...

Hyrax Facts

During World War II, famous anthropologist Louis Leakey was sent to look for some Italian prisoners of war who had escaped from a camp in Kenya. Leakey described that he and his team found the men huddled together. They were cold, hungry, and terrified, and begged "to be taken back, as quickly as possible, to the safety and comfort of the prisoner-of-war camp." All night, horrible screams and screeches had scared them. The terrible beast they imagined turned out to be only small tree hyraxes.

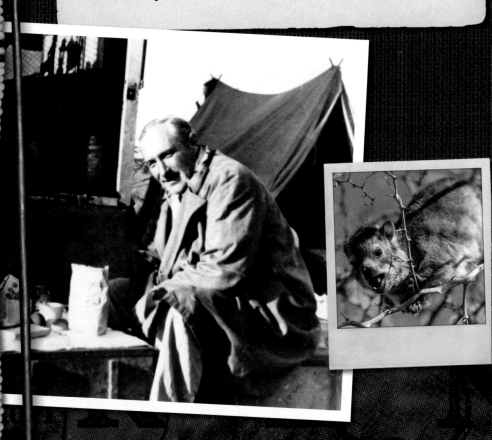

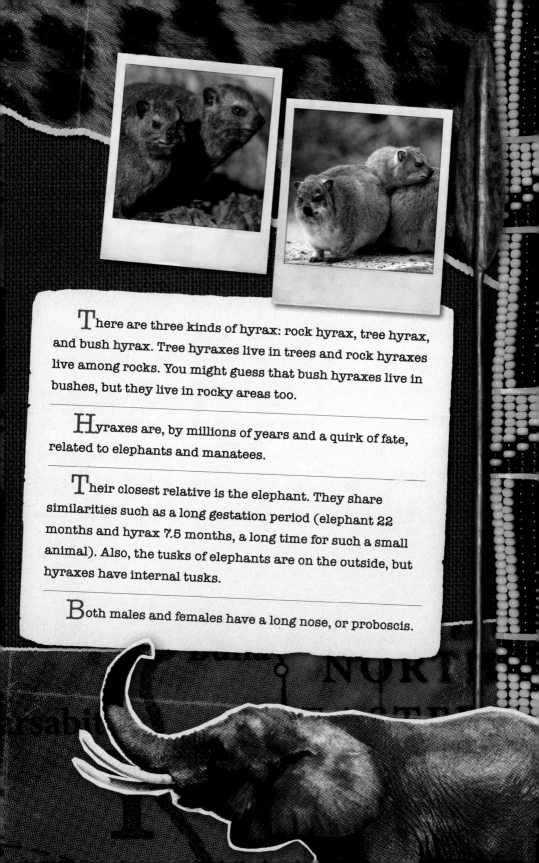

There are three kinds of hyrax: rock hyrax, tree hyrax, and bush hyrax. Tree hyraxes live in trees and rock hyraxes live among rocks. You might guess that bush hyraxes live in bushes, but they live in rocky areas too.

Hyraxes are, by millions of years and a quirk of fate, related to elephants and manatees.

Their closest relative is the elephant. They share similarities such as a long gestation period (elephant 22 months and hyrax 7.5 months, a long time for such a small animal). Also, the tusks of elephants are on the outside, but hyraxes have internal tusks.

Both males and females have a long nose, or proboscis.

13

THE LIFE BETWEEN

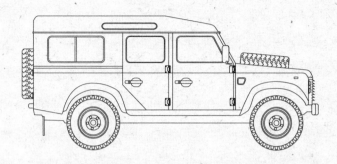

Growing up in the Maasai village of Oltorotua in the Masai Mara, Kenya, our culture grooms young herders to be nature lovers. I grew up herding cattle in an area where wildlife freely roamed. I learned to interact with all the dangerous wildlife, such as lions, buffalo, and elephants. Learning about the behavior of dangerous animals is interesting and also difficult. My older brother Nterere, the Great Herder as I refer to him, taught me how to deal with dangerous animals, including charging elephants.

Some of us herders decided to become professional safari guides. After my high school education, I formalized the skills I learned from herding to become a safari guide. I attended Koiyaki Guiding School in the Masai Mara. Like any college, getting in was not easy. I attended an interview with hundreds of other applicants. Financial aid came from Carl and Mary Kruhm, friends from the USA.

After two years of classwork and field training, I graduated as a Bronze level guide. Three years after, I sat for my Silver level test and passed.

Visitors need a good, experienced guide while on safari. Experienced guides give them details on nature interpretation, cultural values, wildlife names, and animal behaviors, from the smallest insect to giant elephant.

Making a good plan for a day's game drive is also very important. Most visitors are on a tight schedule and they do not want to feel a guide is wasting their time.

Being a guide is one of the most enjoyable jobs a person can have. It gives one a chance to enjoy the gift and beauty of nature. Most interesting is being able to share guiding knowledge with local and international tourists. This becomes a part of conservation efforts if more people are aware of the importance of wildlife and nature itself. This could, in turn, help us preserve our planet and manage our natural resources better. This knowledge can also lead to us finding good solutions for problems such as global warming.

For many decades, men have dominated the guiding profession. As a job that needs both physical and intellectual skills, the stereotype of it being a men's profession existed. This has changed a lot in the last two decades. The Koiyaki Guiding School that I attended is now enrolling an equal number of men and women. Most women have proved the stereotype wrong and they are working as very successful guides.

For Maasai who are not employed in tourists camps in the Mara, life is different. Then we start a day by waking up and preparing for the day's work at Enasirie—as the sun's rays spark the horizon.

A man starts the day by checking the cattle. Entering the cattle kraal first thing in the morning, a standing bull indicates that some mating was happening in the night. This is a good blessing of the day for a Maasai.

My father would go round the kraal to check that all animals were well and there were no signs of entry by predators during the night. My mother would follow closely with gourds ready for early morning milking.

A minute or less later you would see all the women standing by their hut doors. Holding gourds or calabashes for milking is a sign that the day has started well. After milking cattle, the women would go back to their huts for daily household tasks.

One of the young men would be scheduled to be a herder. He would be getting ready for an early single meal for the day. One or two of the boys would accompany him to learn how to be a good herder, someone who protects the family's cattle and other livestock for long hours. None of them take food or drink, but sometimes the young boys gather wild berries to give them energy.

My life is in between the traditional one and my modern job as a guide. I feel lucky to experience both and I am equally proud to be born Maasai and be a guide in the Masai Mara. I am worried that modern life will make many Maasai change their way of living. I believe essential cultural traditions should be preserved.

However, changes such as a good education, better jobs, and saving our wildlife are needed. Historically, the Maasai were known as a warrior tribe, including cattle raids and lion hunts. Both practices have now ceased. Most of the traditional lion hunt areas are now protected wildlife areas such as Masai Mara National Reserve, Serengeti National Park and the many wildlife conservancies in Maasailand. I feel privileged that I can share my knowledge of nature and our cultural pride with the rest of the world.

Karibu—Welcome, visitors, to Kenya, East Africa and experience the magic awaiting!

Buna

NORTH

EASTER

Marsabit

Y A

Waji

isamis

Woyamdero

EASTERN

Plain

Ewaso Ng'iro

Habarwein

Mado Gashi

Lorian

Swamp

Hagadera

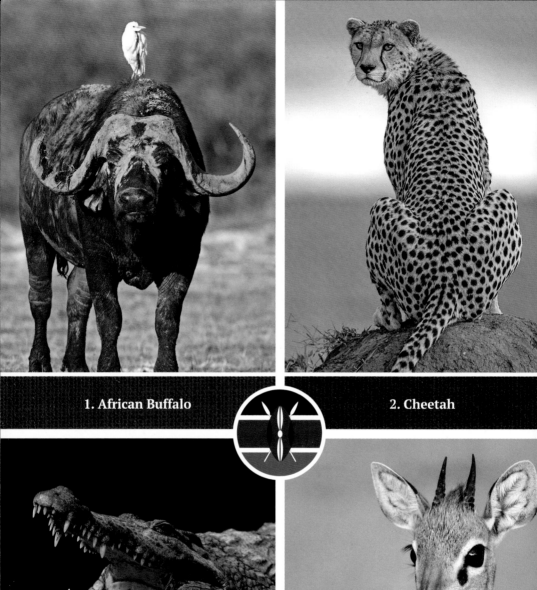

1. African Buffalo

2. Cheetah

3. Crocodile

4. Dik-dik

AN A-Z OF MASAI MARA WILDLIFE

1. **African buffalo:** African or Cape buffalo is one of the Big Five of Africa. Very aggressive; related to the bison, which Americans call buffalo.

2. **Cheetah:** member of cat family and fastest of all animals on land, reach speed of 80 mph.

3. **Crocodile:** large reptile similar to alligator, live in many rivers in Africa.

4. **Dik-dik:** smallest of the antelope family.

5. **Eagle:** bird of prey known for strong hook-like beak and sharp vision for spotting and catching prey.

6. **Eland:** largest of African antelopes; weigh about 1 ton.

7. **Elephant:** African elephant weighs approximately 5–6 tons and is largest mammal on land.

8. **Gazelle:** member of the antelope family.

9. **Giraffe:** tallest animal on land, reaching height of 18-20 feet.

10. **Hippopotamus:** one of biggest killers of people in Africa even though it stays in mostly rivers and swamps.

11. **Hyena:** African predator and scavenger with the strongest jaws and teeth.

12. **Hyrax:** rabbit-like animal related to elephant.

13. **Jackal:** member of dog family.

14. **Leopard:** most elusive African cat; looks like a jaguar.

15. **Lion:** king of the jungle and largest African cat.

16. **Ostrich:** largest African bird; doesn't fly.

17. **Rhinoceros:** an animal about the size of a buffalo with two horns on the forehead made of keratin (compressed hair).

18. **Topi:** antelope with blue markings on hindquarters; stands on termite mounds to look for predators.

19. **Vulture:** bird of prey that scavenges on carrion.

20. **Warthog:** type of wild pig common in Mara

21. **Wildebeest:** commonest animal in the Mara-Serengeti; main animal in the great annual migration across Mara River.

22. **Zebra:** horse-like animal with black and white stripes.

5. Eagle

6. Eland

7. Elephant

8. Gazelle

9. Giraffe

10. Hippopotamus

11. Hyena

12. Hyrax

13. Jackal

14. Leopard

15. Lion

16. Ostrich

17. Rhinoceros

18. Topi

19. Vulture

20. Warthog

21. Wildebeest

22. Zebra

THE MAASAI AND THE MASAI MARA

Kenya's Masai Mara Game Reserve is known around the world as a conservation area with wildlife of all types. A football field in the United States, including the end zones, is 1.32 acres. That means the Masai Mara Game Reserve, which is 583 square miles, covers about 282,667 football fields.

Close your eyes and picture a visit to the Mara. Since most safaris offer three game drives each day—morning, afternoon, and evening—you have time each day to relax and safely watch wildlife from your jeep. In one day you might see several giraffe munching leaves from high up on a tree. Two lions, their manes golden in the sunlight, snooze under another tree. The jeep stops along the dirt road for several minutes while a herd of over twenty elephants crosses the road. "Look right," your guide says, "there are about fifty wildebeest in that herd." Driving on, a line of zebras runs across the open field. Their swishing stripes make them look like an optical illusion. An ostrich, the world's largest bird, can be seen fluffing its feathers. A topi stands atop a termite mound several feet high. Your guide points out a Cape Buffalo barely visible in some leafy bushes. A little later the jeep stops and you walk down to the river, where a baby hippo paddles near its mother. It's been a full day and perhaps tomorrow you'll see crocodile, leopard, cheetah, baboons, rhino, hyena, gazelle, and....

You fall asleep dreaming about the next day's adventure.

This huge reserve has no fences so the park land inside blends into land outside. The entire area is simply called "the Mara," which means "spotted" in Maa.

The Maasai have lived in the Mara for many years. They migrated south from the Nile valley in the Sudan and now live in the central and southwestern part of Kenya, and in northern Tanzania. Although the customs and ways of living differ across this huge area, the ways the Maasai are similar outweigh the differences.

The Maasai were known as fierce fighters but are now a pastoral people who welcome visitors and enjoy explaining their special lifestyle and culture. In remote villages many of the people speak Maa, their tribal language. Those who are safari guides and others in jobs working with the public also speak English and Swahili, the two official Kenyan languages.

The Maasai take pride in being close to the natural world but they also have their own way of life. An English translation of a Maasai prayer asks the Creator to give them children and cattle. Both of these are important to the Maasai.

For a Maasai child, life begins being carried on their mother's back as she goes about her chores. Children don't play with games and toys. Girls join the women in carrying water from the river, learning beadwork, and building a traditional house. They collect firewood and care for younger children. Young boys use sticks to make-believe they are driving cattle and pretend to shoot with a bow and arrow and throw a spear. At about age six, boys begin to pasture cattle. Then, because herders use spears to protect cattle, by age 12 every Maasai boy learns how to use a real spear and help his father with work, like building a fence.

You may see young Maasai men and women in the major towns and cities of Kenya selling animals and goods, like baskets and beaded jewelry. Although the Maasai value keeping their traditional way of life, they are good at finding new ways to use their skills and talents in the world of today.

GLOSSARY

Maa is the word used for the language of the Maasai people. Just as the people of France speak French, people who are Maasai speak Maa. Some of the words below are Swahili, a language used in many countries across east and central Africa.

Big 5: African wild animals that game hunters in the past valued as trophies and were most feared because they were very dangerous to hunt; the five are lion, elephant, leopard, buffalo, and rhino

chui: Swahili word for leopard

enasirie: "as the sun rays sparks horizon": dawn in Maa

enkipai: Maa word for the Mara River

Great Migration: annual mass movement of herbivores, such as wildebeests and zebras in the Mara-Serengeti region of Africa; numbers approximated to be more than 15 million animals

hatari: Swahili word for danger

inoomongo: Maa word used to describe cattle as necessary to feed the tribe; mongo means "the last drop of fresh milk in a gourd"

iswam: Maa word used to describe the love of cows

orripie: a small guardhouse usually slept in by young men and boys while guarding cattle and other small animals

kileken: the bright morning star

Mme tuan: Maasai phrase for "not right or not good"

nailang'a: delicious drink made from mixing cow blood and milk

nkishu: Maa word for cattle

olkinya lasho: "calf-eater," refers to leopard in Maa

safari: Swahili word for "travel" that is commonly used with international tourists traveling to Africa

shuka: bright red, blue, or purple sheet, worn by Maasai tribe members like a cape or wrapped around the body

simba: Swahili word for lion

symbiosis: a mutual relationship between two or more animals

BIBLIOGRAPHY

Reading books like this one and learning more about these unique people help protect and preserve the Maasai culture. Ask a librarian for some recent books and websites about them. Here are a few to start your search.

- Barsby, J. (2017). *Culture Smart! Kenya.* Kuperard Publishers.

- Cutler, J. (2019). *Among the Maasai: A Memoir.* She Writes Press.

- Deedy, C. A., Naiyomah, W. K., & Gonzalez, T. (2016). *14 Cows for America.* Peachtree Press.

- Kingdon, J. (2020). *The Kingdon Pocket Guide to African Mammals.* Princeton University Press.

- Lekuton, J. L. (2005). *Facing the Lion: Growing up Maasai on the African Savanna.* National Geographic Kids.

- Ole Kulet, H. R. (1971). *Is it Possible?* Longman.

- Saitoti, T. O. (1986). *The Worlds of a Maasai Warrior: An Autobiography.* Dorset Press.

- http://www.maasaimara.com

- https://www.outsidego.com/africa-conservation/koiyaki-guiding-school

- https://maasaierc.org

**Jackson Liaram
and Mary Bowman-Kruhm**

In 2004, after a visit to Kenya, Mary Bowman -Kruhm and her family had the opportunity to sponsor Jackson Liaram's education as part of his quest to become a safari guide. This was the beginning of an amazing friendship that has involved working to bring a well to Jackson's village so villagers could have access to water and writing this book. As Mary says, "I am proud that Jackson, as a safari guide, now shares his knowledge of wildlife and passion for protecting it both with visitors to the Mara and with this book. Jackson is truly like a son to me. From knowing him, I have learned how alike all people are. He has shown me 'one finger cannot pinch a louse' (everyone needs other people). In Maa, 'Medany olkimojino obo elashei.'"